The Ride Home

The Ride Home

Gail Anderson-Dargatz

ORCA BOOK PUBLISHERS

Library and Archives Canada Cataloguing in Publication

Title: The ride home / Gail Anderson-Dargatz.
Names: Anderson-Dargatz, Gail, 1963– author.
Series: Orca currents.
Description: Series statement: Orca currents

Identifiers: Canadiana (print) 20190169095 | Canadiana (ebook) 20190169109 |
ISBN 9781459821422 (softcover) | ISBN 9781459821439 (PDF) |
ISBN 9781459821446 (EPUB)

Classification: LCC PS8551.N3574 R53 2020 | DDC jc813/.54—dc23

Library of Congress Control Number: 2019943970
Simultaneously published in Canada and the United States in 2020

Summary: In this high-interest novel for middle readers,
thirteen-year-old Mark adjusts to the long ride home on the school
bus after moving to a small town to live with his grandmother.

*Orca Book Publishers is committed to reducing the consumption
of nonrenewable resources in the making of our books. We make
every effort to use materials that support a sustainable future.*

Orca Book Publishers gratefully acknowledges the support for its publishing
programs provided by the following agencies: the Government of Canada, the
Canada Council for the Arts and the Province of British Columbia through
the BC Arts Council and the Book Publishing Tax Credit.

Edited by Tanya Trafford
Cover artwork by gettyimages.ca/Joseph Devenney
Author photo by Mitch Krupp

ORCA BOOK PUBLISHERS
orcabook.com

Printed and bound in Canada.

23 22 21 20 • 4 3 2 1

For all us rural kids
who endure a long bus ride home

Chapter One

I step into the school bus and stand next to the driver's seat, looking for a place to sit by myself. The bus smells like rotten oranges, sweaty running shoes and cheese. It's the middle of November, and this is my first time on the bus. In fact, this afternoon is the first time I've been on *any* school bus. Back in Vancouver I took public transit, the city buses.

And Gran dropped me off this morning on my first day at this school.

"Keep moving," the driver says. But she doesn't bother to look up from the romance novel she's reading. She's about as old as Gran, in her sixties. And she wears a fedora. Not just a hat. A *fedora*. Like, an old man's hat. I bet she's like that teacher I had in sixth grade who wore a different hat to school every day. A cowboy hat one day, a crown the next. Thinking she's being funny or *fun*. But at least that teacher had pizzazz, energy. This driver appears worn out, like she's been driving the school bus for a while now. Too long. She nods wearily in my general direction. "Take a seat."

Yeah, I think, but where? Most of the seats already have at least one kid in them. Super-little kids, probably kindergartners, sit in the first rows at the front, and what look like elementary kids are just behind them. The ones who look like they're around ten or eleven, younger middle schoolers, take up the middle of the bus. The biggest kids, the cool eighth graders, are at the back.

Seating on the school bus is by age group then, I guess. Well, except for this one girl who's clearly the weird kid. She's about my age, thirteen or so, but is sitting three seats from the front with the young kids. She is wearing glasses, and her hair is bunched into a knot. She has these big headphones on and is reading a book. I can see the title. It's a textbook on how the brain works. A smart kid then.

It's clear that everyone in each little group knows one another. They're friends. I'm arriving at this school late in the fall. Even if I wanted to, which I don't, I doubt I'll make friends now. Who cares? It's not like I'm staying long anyway.

I start to make my way down the aisle. A red-haired girl whispers to another girl, and they giggle at me like I've got my fly open or something. I check. I don't. I feel my face heat up.

"Hey, fresh meat!" some guy shouts.

"What's with the merman hair?" the red-haired girl asks. Oh, so it was my *hair* they were giggling about. There are a few dye jobs on the bus. But nothing like my bright neon green and blue spikes. I just had it done before...well, before.

I ignore them, keeping my eyes on the single empty seat I spotted at the very back. I want nothing to do with these rural freaks. I'm only staying with Gran until Mom gets back on her feet. Then I'm back to the city, first chance I get.

I slide into the empty seat next to the emergency exit. I figure here, at least, I'll be left alone. But then a guy dressed in a black hoodie pulled low over his face turns in his seat to look at me. He's wearing black lipstick. And what little hair I can see is dyed black. His face is pale, like he never sees the sun. There are circles under his eyes like he never sleeps. The guy is the Grim Reaper. All emo.

"Hey, *Merman*. I wouldn't sit there if I were you," he says. "That's Jeremy and Sophie's seat."

Two people couldn't sit here. The seat I'm in and the one on the other side of the emergency exit are only big enough for one person. And anyway, back in the city, nobody "owned" a bus seat. I stare out the window, hoping he will leave me alone.

"Don't say I didn't warn you," says Emo.

My reflection stares back at me. That colorful spiked hair. Ocean-blue eyes (or so Gran tells me). The new puffer jacket

Gran inflicted on me. Warm, but not my style. I look tired, almost as tired as Emo. No, I look *sad*.

I refocus on the school parking lot. It's been snowing since before lunch, the first snow of the season. The school grounds are covered in the stuff. Clouds hang low over the surrounding hills. Winters are gray and depressing here. I remember that from Christmas visits to my granny's. Vancouver is cloudy all winter too, of course. But at least we hardly ever get snow. This first snowfall has turned to slush on the roads and made them slick. A few parents picking up their kids have trouble driving their cars up the hill to the school.

"That's my seat."

I look up to see this muscled guy in a Canadian tuxedo—a jean jacket and jeans—staring down at me. He seems too old to be in middle school. Jeremy, I presume. Behind him a girl with blond hair dipped in green grips his bicep. This must be Sophie.

"*Our* seat," the girl adds.

I wave a hand to object. "But there's only room for one in this seat."

"Exactly," the girl says. So they're a thing.

"Take that seat," I say, pointing at the one on the other side of the emergency exit.

Emo and several of the eighth-grade kids in nearby seats are watching the drama unfold with interest.

"I don't think you understand," Jeremy says. There's a warning in his voice. "You're sitting in *my* seat."

"*Our* seat," Sophie corrects him.

"Seriously?" I ask.

"Out, now!"

"Is there a problem back there, Jeremy?" the driver asks, using the PA system.

"No problem," Jeremy calls back.

"The new kid is just moving out of my seat."

"*Our* seat," Sophie says. It's like there's an echo in here.

"Get a move on," the driver says, her voice booming over the speaker. "We need to get going. The roads are slippery. It will be tough driving today."

"Fine," I say. "Whatever." I sling my backpack over to the other single seat. Then I watch as Jeremy sits in "his" seat. The girl all but sits on top of him, her legs crossways over his lap. She giggles and giggles. Then, *god*, they start to kiss. To avoid looking at them, I peer up at the ceiling, then squint when I realize there is a blob of pudding up there. Hardened, fossilized, but still clearly *pudding*.

My phone buzzes, and I click on *Messages*. Gran.

How are you doing, Mark? Get on the bus okay?

Yeah. We're about to leave.
Made any friends?
No.

And I'm not going to bother, I think of adding. What's the point in trying to make friends? I'll only be here a couple of weeks max. Why would I want to make friends with any of them anyway? Local yokels, the lot of them.

Another message from Gran pops up.

I talked to your mom today.

There is a long pause in which neither of us texts.

Finally the phone vibrates again.

She's okay. But it's going to be a long haul this time.

A long haul. A phrase Gran uses a lot. She means things aren't going to get better any time soon. *Mom* isn't going to get better anytime soon. I refuse to believe that. Because that would mean Mom's stuck in that creepy hospital.

And I'm stuck up here. On Gran's farm in the middle of nowhere. In this crappy small-town school. On this stinking bus.

Ugh. Jeremy and Sophie are making slurping noises in the next seat. I roll my head back and stare up at the petrified pudding on the ceiling. This is going to be a long ride.

Chapter Two

The bus ambles out of town, rocking back and forth down the highway. City transit isn't exactly quiet, but at least people keep to themselves. The kids on this school bus, on the other hand, are *nuts*. Half of them are screaming at each other. The other half are yelling just to make themselves heard as they talk to their friends.

One orange-haired kid is hurling bits of cheese. *Cheese*. The only kids who are quiet and keeping to themselves are the kindergarten kids right up front. Oh, and that weird girl in the third row. She's got these massive headphones, like, noise-canceling headphones. I wish I had a pair.

Gross. Now Jeremy and Sophie are *really* kissing in the seat. I mean, there's tongue action.

Jeremy catches me squinting at them in disgust and disbelief. He stops kissing and gives me the stink eye. "Do you *mind*?" he asks. "A little privacy, please?"

Privacy? On a school bus?

Then he goes back to snogging the girl. That's it. I'm out of here. I grab my backpack and stand up, steadying myself with a hand on the back of a seat as I try to figure out who to sit with. A skinny kid with blue bangs shakes his head. Okay, I won't sit with him. A girl in yoga pants shifts toward the aisle. Her neither then. I take another step forward, but the bus careens around a sharp corner and I tumble over the seat and headfirst into Emo. I find myself cozying up to Mr. Grim Reaper.

Then the driver suddenly brakes, hurling me sideways into the aisle as she turns abruptly into a pullout. She gets out of her seat and stomps down the aisle as I pick myself up. Now that the driver is standing, I realize just how short she is. I'm sure some of the fourth graders are taller than her. But the expression on her face is just plain scary.

"Uh-oh," says Emo.

"Hey!" the driver calls out. "You! New kid!"

"My name is Mark."

"Don't give me lip."

"I wasn't—I was just telling you my name."

She tilts her head up to talk to me. "Argue with me, and you'll get a memo."

"A what?"

Emo nudges me. "You don't want that," he says quietly. "A memo is a note you have to take home. It says you got in trouble. Get three and you could be kicked off the bus. I've got two."

"But I didn't do anything!" I say.

The driver wags a finger at me. "You got up and switched seats while the bus was moving."

"I do that all the time on the city buses."

"School buses?"

"No. City transit."

She pushes back her fedora. "Didn't you read the Bus Riders Code of Conduct?"

"The *what*?"

"The bus rules that the school sent home with you."

I glance back at Jeremy and Sophie. They've stopped making out, for the moment. I suspect they didn't get a copy of the Bus Riders Code of Conduct either. "Nobody sent anything home with me," I tell the driver. "I just started school today. I lived in Vancouver until Friday."

"What happened?" the cheese-hurling kid calls out from several seats down. "You get expelled or something?"

I scowl at him. "None of your business."

But Cheese Kid won't let it go. "No, really. What did you do? You hit a teacher? I bet you hit a teacher."

The driver reaches up to hold a finger to my face. "On this bus, you don't get up and walk around while the bus is moving. Understand?"

"But they were making out back there." I wave a hand at Jeremy and

Sophie. "I didn't want to see *that* all the way home."

"Jeremy, is that true?" the driver asks. "Don't lie to me. All I have to do is review the security footage to find out." She points up at the camera mounted on the ceiling above the emergency exit. Jeremy nods and mumbles. Then he pushes Sophie's legs off his lap, and she falls into the aisle. The girl sheepishly gets up and slides over to the other single seat.

"This isn't the place for that kind of thing," the driver says. "I'm separating you two. Jeremy, go sit in the front seat."

He stands. "With the kindies? No way."

"You want another memo?" the driver asks. "You get a third, and you won't be riding this bus anymore."

"My mom will kill me," Jeremy says.

"Yes, she will." The driver gestures forward with both hands, like a flight attendant. "To the front."

On his way past me, Jeremy slugs my arm. "You'll pay for this," he says.

Once she gets back up front, the driver calls out to me. "And you!" Now that the kids are quiet, watching us, her voice carries all the way to the back of the bus.

"My name is Mark!" I shout back.

The driver snorts. "If I know a kid's name, it's because he keeps getting into trouble. I can see I'm going to remember *your* name. So, *Mark*, if you need to change seats, do it when we stop to let a kid off. But only with my permission. Understand?"

I look back at Jeremy's girl and the empty seat beside her. She glares at me. I'm not sitting back there again. "Can I move now?" I ask the driver.

"Hop to it!" she says.

I slide into the seat with Emo. Even dressed like the Grim Reaper he seems more welcoming than these other kids. At least he tried to warn me not to sit in Jeremy's seat. He lifts his black lip at me. I'm not sure if it's a smile or a sneer. I can't see his eyes under the hoodie. "Hey," I say, in a half-hearted attempt to be friendly.

The driver picks up her mic to finish her lecture. "I don't want any more trouble from any of you. The roads are bad enough today with all the snow. I don't need more distractions. You don't want to be the cause of an accident, do you?" When nobody replies, she raises her voice. "Do you?"

The kids grunt and mumble. I guess they're agreeing. Most of them are now lost in their phones. When the driver settles back in her seat, the screaming and yelling starts up again. A hard eraser pelts me in the back of the head. I see it tumble into the aisle. "Hey!" I say, turning.

Jeremy's girlfriend, Sophie, gives me a nasty smile. I rub my head as I swivel in my seat. But Jeremy is also glaring at me from the front, two rows up from Weird Girl. He's sitting next to a little girl dressed in a princess outfit. As Jeremy hulks there beside her, staring at me, I watch the princess take off her crown and put it on Jeremy's head. He leaves it on as he flips me the bird. Great. All I wanted was to sit by myself and be left alone. I knew I wasn't going to make any friends here. But I didn't think that just ten minutes into this bus ride I would already have enemies.

Chapter Three

I nudge Emo. "How long *is* this bus ride anyway?" I ask him.

He slowly turns my way, and I can finally see his eyes. Once I get past all that white face makeup and black eyeliner, I can see that his eyes are greenish-yellow and puppy-dog sad, like my Gran's Lab's. I wonder what Emo looks like without the makeup and hoodie. Like someone else entirely, I bet.

"The bus ride?" I ask again. "About how long?"

Emo lets out a long sigh, as if I've interrupted him while in some difficult task. Like thinking. "Depends where you get off but about an hour and a half," he says finally. "If Grace is on the bus."

"Grace?"

"That girl who always sits at the front with the little kids. She's sort of, you know, odd."

So I was right. She *is* the weird kid. But if *this* guy thinks she's weird, she must be truly strange.

"She lives way out on the end of Lost Lake Road," says Emo. "If she's not on the bus, then we don't have to go that far. Then it's only an hour's drive."

An *hour*. Back in Vancouver I was home from school in less than ten minutes. "I have to spend more than two hours a day on this noisy, smelly bus?"

"Or longer," Emo says.

"Longer?"

"If Ida has to deal with things."

"Ida?"

"The driver."

"What do you mean, if the driver has to *deal with things*?"

"You'll see." Emo eyes Cheese Kid, who is once again hurling bits of cheddar. Everybody needs a hobby, I guess. "So what *did* you do?" Emo asks me.

I tilt my head at him. "What?" I have no idea what he's talking about.

"To get expelled."

"Who said I got expelled?"

"You moved out here, to the middle of nowhere, from Vancouver, in *November*. Why else would you do that unless you got booted out of school?"

"I don't know. Maybe my mom got a job up here. Maybe I came here for the view. Maybe an alien spacecraft dropped me off."

"Is that what happened?"

I peer at him. He seems serious. Is he stoned? "You really think aliens left me here?" I ask.

"No, I mean the bit about your mom getting a job here."

"No."

"So why *did* you move up here then?"

I stare past him at the thick snow-flakes that are falling even faster now. I don't want these hicks knowing my story. I don't want to talk to them, period. "Stuff went down," I say.

"I hear ya." Emo nods, but he keeps talking. "My brother got expelled."

I put in my earbuds and fiddle with my phone, picking tunes, thinking this will shut him up. I sat with Emo because I figured he'd be the brooding type. You know, quiet. And, well, he seemed like the only one willing to sit with me. But he just keeps talking.

"He set the school Christmas tree on fire last year."

I pull out one bud, thinking I hadn't heard him right. "Seriously?" I ask. "Your brother set the Christmas tree on fire?" I mean, who does that? Maybe the Grinch.

Emo, suddenly animated, nods his head up and down. "It was *cool*."

"Okay..." I say slowly.

"I wish I could get expelled."

I lift my eyebrows and shake my head slowly, but he doesn't notice. His face has lit up, and he's lost in his happy memory of the burning Christmas tree. Wow.

"You like fires?" he asks.

"What do you mean?" I'm starting to really worry about this guy.

"Fires, explosions. You know, watching things burn and blow up?"

"I used to watch *MythBusters* when I was a kid. So yeah, I guess."

Emo pulls out a lighter and flicks it on and off. "I like watching things burn."

I glance nervously at the driver, Ida. I can see her tired face in the big rearview mirror. "Are you really allowed to carry lighters on the bus?" I ask Emo.

"Are you kidding?" he says. "We're not allowed to carry *anything* cool on the bus. No lighters. No knives. No firecrackers. Nothing that could explode."

I shift a little to the left, toward the aisle. So what else is this guy carrying? "You smoke?" I ask, trying to gauge just how crazy this guy is. "That why you're carrying a lighter?"

"No way. Smoking is bad for your health."

Unlike knives or explosives, I think.

He flicks the lighter again and again. "I just like watching the flames, seeing things burn."

"Yeah, you said that." I scoot as close to the edge as I can without falling out of my seat. When I accidently bump his arm, the kid in the seat across the aisle shifts away and grunts like a caveman. He's got this head of wild, unkempt hair, and he's already got stubble on his chin. The guy sitting next to him could be his brother, his twin even. They both seem like the kind who punch holes in the wall when they're mad. I shift a little back in Emo's direction and scan the middle seats, hoping to spot another place to sit. Someplace less... life-threatening.

"When's the next stop?" I ask.

But Emo is focused on his lighter, flicking it on and off. "I'm guessing these vinyl seats aren't *really* flammable," he says. "You'd think they wouldn't make school-bus seats out of stuff that burns, right?"

"Yeah," I say, my voice cracking a little. "You'd think."

"But watch. All I have to do is hold the flame to the back of the seat, like this—"

"Ah. You think that's a good idea?"

"And it burns, just like that."

The vinyl on the seat doesn't really burn. A hole opens in the upholstery as the material sort of melts away in the flame. But it quickly stops "burning."

"Should you be doing that?" I ask, my voice all at once high and squeaky. "I mean, you could start a fire, in a bus full of kids. We could, you know, *die*."

"Nah," he says. "The vinyl is flame-resistant. It won't catch fire." He blows away a whiff of smoke. "I don't think so anyway." Then he offers me the lighter. "You want to try?"

"God, no!"

"Fire is so cool." The kid flicks the lighter again, presses it to the vinyl and watches as another hole appears. The back of the seat in front of us is full of holes. This must be Emo's favorite seat.

"I think you should stop," I say. "I mean, setting the bus on fire is, you know, kind of dangerous." A lot dangerous.

"Nah, we do it all the time," says Emo. "Don't we, guys?"

He leans forward to peer across the aisle at the cavemen. They bob their heads in unison and, together with Emo, pull out their lighters, flicking them into flame. I start to panic and stare wide-eyed out the front window, hoping vainly that we'll stop soon. But we're still on the highway, miles away from the turnoff to the gravel road that most of the kids live along.

Both cavemen burn a hole into the seat in front of them. Emo nods in approval. "Cool," he says. The smell of burning vinyl starts to fill the back of the bus.

Chapter Four

I peer at the driver's face in the rearview mirror, willing her to smell the smoke so I don't have to say anything. She'll have to stop the bus then, and I'll be able to move away from these clowns. But Emo and then one of the cavemen open the windows on either side of the bus. The cold, snowy air blows the smoke right outside.

Emo flicks his lighter into flame and holds it up to my face. "What's the matter, *Mark*?" he taunts. "You seem nervous." The cavemen grunt and flick their lighters in my direction. The kids around us don't even seem to notice. They just go on screaming or yelling or playing games on their phones.

Then Emo leans even closer. "I bet that spiky green hair of yours would *really* burn."

My heart skips a beat. I don't want to die here, on this frickin' bus. I wave a hand at Ida, the driver. "Ah, excuse me?" I call out. "I think we have a problem here."

"What is it now, *Mark*?" she says through the mic.

"Um, these kids are trying to set the bus on fire—"

"What are you *doing*?" Emo hisses.

"And my hair too," I add.

"*What*?" The driver pulls the bus to the side of the highway.

Emo elbows me hard in the ribs. "*Snitch*."

I whisper back to him, "But you were threatening to set me on *fire*!"

"I was only joking," says Emo. "I'm not like my *brother*. Everybody knows that." The kids in the seats closest to us nod their heads at me like I'm an idiot.

The two cavemen quickly hide their lighters as the driver marches down the aisle. Ida stops and holds out her hand in front of Emo. "Give me that lighter!"

He smiles, trying to appear innocent. But the Grim Reaper hoodie, black lipstick and eyeliner make it hard to pull that off. "What lighter?" he asks.

"The one in your pocket." She stares at Emo until he finally slaps it on her palm. "That's a memo for you, Eric," she tells him. "Your third, as I recall. This is your last ride."

"You've got to be kidding me," says Emo. "If I can't take the bus, how will I get to school?"

I tilt my head at him. "But I thought you said you wanted to get expelled."

"Not for real," he says. "I've got plans. I'm going to get an engineering degree. I can't get into university unless I finish high school."

I figure he likely won't get into university if he keeps burning stuff either.

"Let's go," Ida tells him. "Up to the front."

Finally. A seat to myself.

I get out of the way as Emo stands to his full height. The kid is tall. Taller than me even. The driver follows him as he slumps down the aisle, his black hood still up. Several of the kindergarten kids go wide-eyed in horror as he approaches. Maybe they're thinking he really is the Grim Reaper.

Emo takes the seat in the first row opposite Jeremy and the little girl dressed in the princess outfit. He looks back at me and makes a gesture like he's clicking his lighter. In response, his two caveman buddies beside me pull out their lighters and flick them at me. But they do it behind the seat, so the driver can't see them. "I bet that backpack of yours is pretty flammable," the first caveman says.

I wave at the driver. "Ah, Ida?" I shout. "Okay if I move again?"

"Be quick about it! We've got to get back on the road. The snow is getting worse."

I shift down several rows to the middle of the bus. There I nudge the Cheese Kid to move over. Somehow he now seems to be the sanest of the bunch. "Want one?" he asks, offering me a cheese curd.

Jeremy is still wearing the little

girl's tiara. As the kindie hangs a necklace around his neck, he shakes his head slowly at me, narrowing his eyes. Mr. Grim Reaper just looks, well, grim. I am *so* in for it.

As the driver pulls back out onto the snowy highway, Cheese Kid hurls some cheese curds back at a group of girls. He apparently has an endless supply of cheese products. In response, the girls pull out their yogurt tubes and start flicking them at him. I feel a glob of yogurt splat me in the side of the face. "Hey!" I say.

"Sorry," one of the girls says. "I was aiming for Chucky." The cheese kid's name is Chucky? Like that Chuck E. Cheese kids' restaurant? It's got to be a nickname. It's just too perfect. His hair is orange. And his T-shirt is the same orange as that powdered cheese that comes with the boxed mac and cheese. Cheese is clearly his thing.

"Hey, new kid," he says to me. "Mark

the Merman. I see you've been making friends." He lifts his chin at Jeremy and Emo, who are still glaring at me from their seats.

"I don't want any more trouble," I say. "I just want to be left alone."

"That's going to be tough in a bus full of kids, right?"

Yeah, but it's never a problem on a city bus. I can be alone in a bus so crowded I've got to ride standing, hanging on to a bar. Everyone ignores everyone else, even as we're forced to stand there smelling each other's armpits. And no one throws cheese. Or yogurt. Or tries to set the bus seats—or me—on fire.

"You were expelled from your last school, eh?" Chucky Cheese asks.

"No, I was *not* expelled."

"What are you doing here then? Why are you starting school at, like, the end of November?"

"Why is everyone here so nosy?"

The kid blinks at me with lashes so blond they're almost invisible. "Just asking," he says. I notice his face is covered in freckles. He tosses a cheese curd up in the air and catches it in his mouth. I can hear it squeak against his teeth as he chews. "My parents moved me here last January," Chucky says. "It sucked."

So Chucky Cheese has been here less than a year. But he fits right in. Or maybe he's what this evil bus turns newcomers into—cheese-curd hurlers. I have to get out of here, quick.

"And you're coming from Vancouver?" he asks, chewing another curd. "Moving here must *really* suck then."

"Yeah, well, this is the last place I wanted to go. I mean, I love my granny and everything—" Crap, I shouldn't have admitted I moved in with Gran.

"You live with your grandma? That *seriously* sucks."

I shake my head. "Nah, she's okay." She's kind of cool, actually. She sews costumes for a living. Dance outfits, Halloween getups, theater wardrobes. She ships the clothes to customers all over the place, through her website shop. Her Elvis-impersonator costumes are her biggest sellers. Go figure.

In fact, Gran taught my mom to sew. Now Mom has her own home business too. She has a specialty-clothing line, making each dress by hand. Or at least she did. I have no idea what's going to happen now.

"So where are your parents?" Emo asks. "They move in with your granny too?"

"No."

"Away on business?"

"No."

"On holiday?"

"No."

"Are they dead?"

"No!"

"In the army?"

"No."

"Spies?"

"No!" I scowl at him. "What are you? Some kind of detective?"

Chucky pushes his face close to mine. He smells like cheese. Big surprise. "Did they give you up because you have some kind of weird disease?" he asks. "Like that flesh-eating disease? Are you all gross and contagious? Am I going to catch something just from talking to you?"

"*No!*" God, this kid is relentless. He just won't give up. I sigh. "My dad lives in Toronto, okay?"

"So why didn't you go live with him?"

Good question. If I *had* gone to live with him, I wouldn't be here, in hell, right now.

Chapter Five

I stare out at at the snow sliding sideways on the bus windows. "So...?" asks the cheese kid.

"So what?"

"Why didn't you go live with your dad?"

What can I tell this kid that will shut him up? Dad hasn't been in my life for years. I get cards with money in them on my birthday and at Christmas. He remarried and has a whole other family. I have a half sister and half brother I've never met. When things got hard with my mom, he just left. "I don't know him very well," I say finally.

"What about your mom? Is she dead?"

"No." I try to ignore Chucky, but he keeps staring at me until I can't take it anymore. "My mom got sick, okay?" I say. This wasn't the first time either. Every time Mom gets sick, I stay with Gran. And I've stayed with Gran a lot—every Christmas and summer and whenever Mom needs a break. But up until now those visits have only been for a week or two at a time.

Chucky leans in, like he's hoping for some big secret. "What kind of sick?"

I don't answer.

"Does she have, like, cancer or something?"

"No."

"Heart attack? Stroke?"

"No."

"Grace's mom had a stroke. Now she talks funny." Chucky lifts his chin toward the weird girl.

Well, that news about her mom explains why Grace is reading a book on how the brain works. "*That* sucks," I say.

"Grace used to sit here with us, in the middle of the bus. After her mom got sick, she started sitting up front with the kindies."

Now that I know what this bus is like, I figure Grace made the right choice.

The girls squirt more yogurt our way. A blob oozes down my shoulder. Chucky Cheese kneels on his seat to lob more cheese. The girls toss more yogurt. And then out come the pudding cups. When squeezed just so, pudding cups can spray straight up to the ceiling. And it turns out nearly every kid on the bus has a pudding cup, like they've been saving them just for this. Gobs of pudding rain down. I hold my hands up over my head so pudding won't get in my hair. Now I know why Emo keeps his hoodie up all the time.

"Stop that! Stop it right now!" The bus driver yells through the mic. Then she stops the bus *again*. Once she has pulled over, she marches down the aisle. "Who started this?" she yells. "Come on, out with it!" Her face is red. A vein in her neck pulses.

"It was the new kid," somebody shouts.

Ida glares down at me. "*Mark*?"

"It wasn't me! I don't even have pudding," I say. "I didn't bring a lunch!"

"You didn't have *lunch*?" Ida seems worried, and I wonder if she's about to offer me a granola bar or something.

"I brought money for lunch," I say. "Like I always do."

"Well," she says, sniffing. "Isn't it nice that some of us can afford to buy lunch every day."

"I don't—I'm not rich."

But she isn't listening. She's still after the culprit. She eyes Chucky.

"Don't look at me," he says. "I don't have pudding." He holds up a bag of curds. "I have cheese."

"He really likes cheese," one of the kids says.

Oh, ya think? He likes throwing cheese, at least.

The driver pushes on down the row, interrogating each of the kids. But no one confesses to the first pudding squirt or to squirting pudding, period, even though the bus is now dripping with the stuff.

"All right," she says finally. "You'll *all* clean up the pudding."

There's a collective groan from the kids as Ida goes back to her seat to grab some paper towel. She rips off sheets and hands them to everyone. I take mine and wipe the pudding off my shoulder before tackling the ceiling.

So *this* is what Emo meant when he said the ride home takes longer when Ida "has to deal with things."

"Does something like this happen every day?" I ask Chucky.

"Pretty much."

I sigh and accidentally catch Weird Girl's—I mean, Grace's—eye as she cleans pudding off the back of her seat. She raises one eyebrow and gives me a look as if to say, *Can you believe this*?

Suddenly *she* seems like the sanest kid on the bus. The safest anyhow, even if she is sitting only two rows down from Jeremy and Emo. I can see now why she chooses to sit so close to the driver.

Then, *god*, Chucky uses his *pudding* to draw on the window. He draws a… not sure I should say what. Let's just say it rhymes with Venus. On the window. With *pudding*.

Okay, that's it. I've had enough of Chucky. The kid is gross and a walking food fight. I head down the aisle, ducking the pudding-covered balls of paper towel kids are now lobbing around the bus.

I stop at the weird girl's seat. Grace's seat. "Okay if I sit here?" I ask.

"Sure," she says. "But do you think that's a good idea right now?" She nods at Jeremy and Emo.

Emo is leaning across the aisle, showing Jeremy something on his phone. They both smile back at me, like they've got something on me.

I drop my backpack on the floor. "I'm assuming we're sitting close

47

enough to the driver that those two won't chance—anything."

"I wouldn't count on it," she says. But she shifts so I can sit. "I'm Grace," she says.

"Mark," I say.

"I know," she says, smiling a little. She's got a nice smile. "So you're from Vancouver?"

I shrug. "I just want to sit here and listen to my tunes, okay?"

She looks hurt. "Yeah, sure," she says.

I put in my earbuds and close my eyes. But as soon as I do, I feel a wet, gooey ball of paper towel hit me square in the face. I open my eyes to see Jeremy laughing. Emo lobs his own pudding ball at me. I manage to grab it before it hits me. I juggle it a moment before I start to throw it back. But Grace puts a hand on my arm.

"I wouldn't," she says. "You'll only make things worse for yourself. And do you really want to be like them?" She glances first at Jeremy and Emo, then at the madhouse behind us. Balls of wadded paper towels are flying everywhere. I watch as one knocks the driver's hat off. Ida waves her arms in the air, screaming for the kids to stop.

"No," I say, keeping my eyes on Jeremy and Emo. They're practically daring me to throw it back. I know it's a trap. They're baiting me. They have something planned for me.

"I just want to go home," I say. Then I realize it's not Gran's place I'm thinking of. I want to go *home* to Vancouver.

The homesick feeling is an ache that rises from my belly to my throat. But it's not so much for the condo I share with my mom. I want to go back to the life that I had *before* Mom took those pills this last time. I want to go back to the way things were.

Chapter Six

Ida finally pulls out a whistle. A
whistle! And blows it. Hard. The shrill
sound makes everyone stop what
they're doing and cover their ears. She
blows it again and motions for everyone
to get back in their seats. For once the
bus is quiet. Grace suddenly relaxes
beside me, and I realize then just how
tense the noise was making me too.

"Now that I have your attention," the driver yells, "let me make myself perfectly clear. The next kid who throws pudding or yogurt or cheese or anything else gets a memo. And if you think you can sneak it past me, think again. I *will* be reviewing the security-camera footage tonight. I expect you to sit still in your seats, stare straight ahead and behave yourselves."

Ida points out the window at the heavy snow that's falling. Her face is an alarming red. "The driving conditions are terrible. I'm having trouble keeping this bus on the road. The last thing I need is you hooligans taking my attention away from driving. It's my job to keep you all safe. You *will* behave. Or I'll end up having an accident and it will be *your* fault. Is that understood?"

There are a few grumbles and mutters.

Ida raises her voice. "Do you *understand*?"

A few kids say, "Yes, Ida." Others just scroll or text on their phones. But no one is throwing anything. No one is even talking now. After the racket of the last twenty minutes, the quiet is a relief.

Ida pushes her way back up the aisle and gets in her seat. She grips the steering wheel with her head bowed for a moment. Then she pulls the bus back onto the highway.

I elbow Grace as I nod at the driver. "I hope they pay her well," I say.

"Are you kidding?" she says. "They could never pay her enough for this job."

She's got a point. I'm just happy Ida's outburst has put a damper on whatever revenge Jeremy and Emo were plotting. They're both facing forward now, though I can see Emo's black-rimmed eyes peering at me through the big rearview mirror.

He makes a gesture like he's flicking his lighter again. I nervously run a hand through the spikes of my hair. He only stops staring at me when Jeremy takes the little girl's tiara and slaps it on top of Emo's hoodie. Emo takes it off, inspects it and puts it back on. An interesting fashion statement. Sort of Goth meets *Frozen*.

Grace goes back to reading her book on the brain. But she doesn't bother to put her noise-canceling headphones on.

I pull out my phone and check for messages. Gran has sent me several more.

Your mom sent her love.

She misses you.

You should phone her.

The thing is, I don't know if I can do that. Phone Mom, I mean. I wouldn't know what to say. What I really want to ask will only make things worse. *Why did you decide to leave me like that?*

Gran texts again. **She's worried about you.**

Grace leans over. "You'll have to tell your mom the bus is never on time. Or she'll worry."

"It's not my mom. It's Gran."

"Oh. My mom was always freaking out when I first started taking this bus. Every day at least one kid gets in trouble, and Ida has to deal with it. Or we have to stop at the train crossing."

"There's a train crossing? How long would we have to wait for a train to go by?"

Grace tucks a strand of hair behind her ear. "Depends on how long the train is. The last time we stopped at the train crossing, we were sitting so long that Chucky went berserk and tried climbing out the window. And one of the kindies actually peed her pants." She turns the page of her book. I see a picture of a pickled brain in a jar. "But if Ida doesn't have to stop to give a kid heck before we get to the crossing, then we usually beat the train. We don't have to wait."

"*Are* there days like that? When a kid *doesn't* get in trouble?"

"No."

A cheese curd lands in my lap. I flick it to the floor. "So I guess we'll be waiting at the train tracks today."

"You'll get used to it," says Grace. "My mom just expects the bus to be late every day." She holds up her book. "And I bring reading material."

"Late *every* day? Just how late?"

"Don't worry. We usually get home in time for supper." She stops to think about that for a moment. "Most days."

Most days? In time for *supper*? I do the math. Getting home just in time for supper means a *two-hour* bus ride home. Or more. One way. That's four hours a day on this bus. Four hours!

And that's only because almost nobody on this bus knows how to sit still and behave in a moving vehicle. I'm starting to hate these kids. Except Grace. She seems okay. At least she sits still. And doesn't throw cheese or yogurt or pudding. Or draw rude pictures on the window. Oh yeah, or threaten to set my hair on fire.

"You're not so weird," I tell her. Then I cringe. That didn't come out right.

Grace pushes her glasses up. "Gee, thanks."

"I didn't mean it like that."

"How did you mean it?"

How do I dig myself out of this one? "You sit up here with the kindies, so I thought—" I wasn't sure what I thought. "And that emo guy said you were odd, and he's, like, *strange*. I figured if *he* thought you were weird, then you really must be." I look back at Chucky, who has two cheese curds tucked under his top lip, like buck teeth. "But it's all these other kids who are weird."

"Eric," she says quietly.

"What?"

"Emo guy. His name is Eric. And he's not emo exactly." She thinks about that for a moment. "Well, maybe he is. But he's okay. He's just—"

"Into burning things." I can't believe Grace is defending this guy.

"I was going to say he's just had a hard time. His dad's always on his case. Eric has come to school with a black eye a few times."

"From his dad?"

Grace glances at Eric to make sure he's not listening and nods.

"Huh. Seems like everyone on this bus has a story."

"Well, duh. All people do."

She's right, of course. I've been quick to judge. "I guess I know why you sit up here with the kindergarten kids," I say. "The same reason I ended up here, I bet. To escape the insanity. Or did you get in trouble?"

She shakes her head. "I chose to sit here." She points a thumb behind her. "To avoid *that*."

"You'd think the kindergarten kids would be the noisy ones," I say.

"The sixth- and seventh-grade kids on this bus are the worst."

She's got that right.

"And I get carsick. If I sit here, I can look out the front window when I need to. Stops me from barfing."

"Always good," I say, leaning away from her.

She smiles at my joke. "You live with your grandma?" she asks.

"You heard, huh?"

"You mentioned your gran. And the kids passed it down the rows. Along with something about your dad being a spy?"

59

I smile and shake my head. "He's not a spy. My dad has the most boring job on the planet. He's an insurance salesman."

"And your mom?"

I don't want to talk about my mom. I don't want to think about my mom. Thinking about her makes me remember her on the floor of our kitchen. Then I feel the panic I felt while I checked her pulse and phoned 9-1-1. The empty feeling in my gut as I realized what she had done.

Chapter Seven

Grace elbows me. "You okay?" she asks.

"Yeah, I'm fine."

"You kind of zoned out there when I asked about your mom."

"Just tired, I guess," I say. "First day at a new school and all that. And then *this*." I wave a hand at the kids on the bus, hoping she will let it go. But no such luck.

"Is she sick or something?" she asks. "Your mom?"

I've already offered up more of my life to this busload of kids than I wanted to. So I start shooting *her* questions. "I heard your mom had a stroke. That right?"

"A few months back. She used to run marathons. Now I have to help her climb the stairs."

"I'm sorry."

Grace fiddles with a folded corner on the page of her book. "It's okay. She's getting better." But then she looks so sad that I feel like I should offer her something.

I take a deep breath. "My mom," I say finally, "she's sick too." I figure that isn't giving much away. Chucky Cheese has already got that out of me.

"Sick how?"

"Just sick."

Grace keeps her eyes on me, trying to figure me out, I guess. She's kind of pretty in a nerdy sort of way. Her eyes under those glasses are a deep brown, framed by long eyelashes. Her skin is zit-free, unlike almost every other middle-school kid on this bus. Me included.

"You're not the only one living with a grandma, you know," she says.

"Oh?"

"Eric is too now."

"Emo guy?" The Grim Reaper lives with his *grandma*? Doesn't seem likely somehow.

"Eric," she corrects me. "His name is Eric."

Right. *Eric*.

At the sound of his name, Eric scowls at us. He's still wearing the princess crown on top of his hoodie.

After he turns away, Grace lowers her voice. "He just left home," she says. "He couldn't live with his dad anymore. His granny took him in."

"Huh." Who knew? I have something in common with this guy.

Grace closes her book. I guess we're having a conversation whether I want to or not.

"I'm sorry you had to leave your school like that."

"Not your problem."

"I mean, I know what it's like."

"You live with your grandma too?" I ask.

"No. But my mom remarried a few years ago, and my brother and I had to move here with her. I hated it for a long time. I kept thinking maybe Mom would break up with Bryan. That's my stepdad. Or maybe she and Dad would get back together. I just wanted to move back to Calgary and to the way things were. I didn't want to make friends here because that would mean I was giving up on my old life."

I guess she *does* know what it's like. I don't want to make friends at school or on this bus. If I do, I'll have to admit I'm here for good. And that things have changed.

"I know what you mean—" I start. But then Jeremy and Eric both turn in their seats.

"Hey, Fresh Meat," Jeremy calls.

"Mark the Merman," Eric corrects him.

"Want to play a little truth or dare?"

I look at Grace. She'll know if this is a bad idea.

But Jeremy isn't waiting. "You know how it goes. You choose if we ask you a question or dare you to do something."

I see Ida lift her chin to study us in the rearview mirror. I shake my head. "Oh, I don't think—"

"We *all* play," says Jeremy. He points at Grace with his phone. "Your girlfriend can play too."

"She's not my girlfriend."

"She won't play," says Eric. "She never plays."

"Truth," Grace says. I get the impression she's trying to deflect their attention away from me.

"Oh, so you've decided to play for once," says Eric.

"*Truth*," Grace says again, more forcefully this time.

"All right," says Jeremy. "So, Grace, do you like the new kid?"

"Mark?" she asks.

Jeremy grins. Maybe he's thinking she'll resist answering, get embarrassed. But Grace lifts her chin. "Yes," she says.

"I like Mark. He seems like a decent guy. Not like the rest of the idiots on this bus."

"Hey, I'm just being friendly here," Jeremy says.

"Okay, Mark's turn," says Eric. "Truth or dare?"

"Oh, I don't know."

"Truth," Grace answers for me. Then she whispers, "Believe me, you don't want to take one of their dares."

"Truth," I say.

"Truth it is," says Eric. "So, *Merman*, why did you move up here? And remember, you have to tell the truth."

"Like I told the cheese kid—"

"Chucky," Grace says.

"I didn't *move* here. I'm only staying with Gran for a bit, until Mom gets back on her feet."

"What's wrong with her? Does she have cancer?" Jeremy asks.

"No."

"Diabetes, heart attack, stroke?" Eric asks. But he's got this sly grin on his face, like he knows something that I don't.

"God, what's with the questions?" I ask. "You're worse than Chucky."

Eric grins, his teeth extra white against those black lips. "So what is it then? Is your mom a *junkie*?"

My heart skips a beat.

"Has she got addiction issues?"

I pause. "No."

"Eric," Grace says. "Come on. Don't be a jerk."

But Eric keeps pushing. "But something like that, right?"

"No!" I slump down in my seat with my arms crossed. "I don't want to play this stupid game."

"Remember, you have to tell the truth. If you don't, there are *consequences*—"

I'm not sure I want to know what he means by that.

Ida eyes us through the rearview mirror. "*Boys*," she warns.

I hold up both hands. "I don't want any trouble," I say.

Jeremy leans into the aisle, lowering his voice to a near whisper. "If that's the case, then you shouldn't have told Ida about Sophie and me kissing in the back."

"She would have seen you," I say, lowering my voice to match his. "I mean, you weren't exactly trying to hide anything."

"You're a snitch," Eric whispers from under his hoodie. "Ida took away my lighter. That's my third memo. I can't ride the bus anymore."

"Why would you want to?" I ask. "This bus is a madhouse."

"A *madhouse*," says Eric. "That's an interesting choice of words."

I feel my stomach drop. "What do you mean?"

"I texted my grandma, asked a few questions. Because she knows *your* gran. And she knows why you're here."

Crap.

I'm about to tell him to get lost when the bus gears down. There's a train crossing at the bottom of a steep hill. The hill is icy, and the bus skids a little as it comes to a stop. The sanding trucks haven't made it to this road yet. With an early snowstorm like this, I guess all the sanding trucks are on the highways.

"Why are we stopping?" I ask Grace. "I don't see a train."

"School buses have to stop at train tracks even if there's no train coming," she replies.

The kids in the back start screaming louder than usual. Grace turns to see what the commotion is about. "Oh, *crap!*" she says.

I turn to see a van skidding down the hill behind us. It spins out of control, then slams right into the back of the bus. The whole bus shakes with the impact and shudders forward on the icy road. I'm flung out into the aisle, and I break my fall with my right hand. When I try to stand, my whole arm burns. Then I see that the collision has pushed the bus onto the tracks. And Ida is hunched over the steering wheel, unconscious.

Chapter Eight

The whole bus is in chaos, even more than before. The kindergarten kids are crying. So are many of the elementary kids. Ida is still slumped over the wheel. There's blood on her forehead. She must have banged her head when the van hit the back of the bus.

"You okay?" Grace asks me.

"Yeah," I say, holding my arm. "But I think our driver is hurt."

"We have a bigger problem," she says. "The front of the bus is sitting on the train tracks." She stands and shouts at the kids behind us. "Someone phone 9-1-1 and tell them we're stuck on the tracks!"

Immediately every kid with a phone starts punching numbers.

"Sophie?" Grace calls. "You okay back there?"

Sophie, still sitting at the very back, looks rattled, but she nods.

"Everyone else okay? Can you walk?" Grace asks.

The kids nod.

"Okay then. I need you all to stay calm and listen to me. Everything is going to be fine."

I am super impressed.

Grace pushes past me and heads right down to the front of the bus.

She checks on Ida and then turns to Jeremy and Eric. "You two lead the kids off the bus by the emergency exit at the back. Take them over to that clearing. Make sure the older kids buddy up with the younger ones. Mark, help me get Ida off the bus. We'll use the front door."

When Jeremy and Eric don't jump up immediately, Grace claps her hands. "Quickly!" she says. "Get the kids off the bus. The train could be here any moment."

I half expect Jeremy and Eric to tell Grace to piss off. But they both start leading the kindergarten kids to the back of the bus. And they do it well, reassuring the little kids and keeping order. It's like they've practiced for this emergency or something.

Grace reaches for the mic on the two-way radio and clicks it on. "Hello, hello," she says. "We have an emergency. A van crashed into the back of the bus, and the bus is now stuck on the train tracks on Church Road."

A voice crackles over the radio. "This is Dispatch. Are the kids off the bus? Please advise."

Grace and I turn and see Eric helping the last kid jump out the back exit of the bus. "Yes, the kids are safe," Grace tells the dispatcher, like she knows exactly what she is doing. "But the driver is injured. We've called 9-1-1, but you need to stop the next train."

We watch Eric and Jeremy follow the kids as they walk in single file over to the clearing. I'm amazed at how calm and orderly they all are. Especially after how they behaved on the ride here.

"Can she be moved?" asks the dispatcher.

Ida groans.

"I think so," Grace says. "She hit her head pretty hard and seems to be unconscious. But I don't see any other injuries. We're going to try to get her off the bus."

"Hurry then," the voice says. "Get yourself to safety. Help is on the way."

Grace puts the radio mic back in place and leans over our driver. "Ida?" she says. Then louder: "Ida!"

Our driver mumbles, groggy.

"Do you know what happened?" Grace asks her.

"What?" Ida says.

"Do you know where you are?"

"I'm in hell," Ida says and grins.

"We've got to get you off the bus," Grace tells her. "The bus slid onto the train tracks."

"What?" Ida squints as she tries to understand what's going on. "The kids! Oh god. I think I'm going to be sick." Ida doubles over, like she's going to barf right there. Then she holds her head like she's in pain.

"Confusion, headache, nausea."
Grace looks up at me. "She probably
has a concussion. Help me get her out
of here." She tries to undo the buckle
on Ida's seat belt. "Great. This is stuck."
Grace reaches above the driver and
takes down a weird-shaped knife.

"What's that?" I ask.

"A seat-belt cutter."

"Seriously?"

"It's here for emergencies. And I'd
say this is an emergency."

"Here, let me help," I say, taking the
cutter from her. Once I've cut through the
seat belt, Grace and I haul Ida to her feet
and down the steps of the bus. Then we
each put a shoulder under her arm and,
together, help her over to the clearing.

"How did you know how to do all
that stuff?" I ask Grace as we walk.

"Everyone on this bus does. We
have this safety stuff grilled into us at

the start of every school year. And we have emergency drills a couple of times a year. A kindie could handle this."

"Really? I doubt that."

"No, it's true. We all know this stuff inside and out. That's why everybody listened when I reminded them what to do."

I suddenly have a new respect for these rural kids. I wouldn't have had a clue what to do.

We lower Ida onto a log. Grace looks over the accident scene as she takes off her coat. The driver of the van is still in her vehicle. An elderly woman. She's clinging to the steering wheel and staring at the school bus in front of her. "I've got to get that lady out of there," Grace says.

"And I've got to let Gran know what's going on," I say. "She'll freak out if she hears about this on Twitter."

I try to text with my right hand, my dominant hand. But that makes my arm hurt. I give up and use my left hand.

Will be late. Bus had accident. I'm okay.

Sort of, I think. My arm feels like it's on fire. When I move my fingers, my forearm feels...wrong. I try to shake it out, but that only makes it worse.

"What's with your hand?" Grace asks as she tucks her coat around Ida.

"I don't know. I broke my fall with this hand. Now my arm burns."

"Let me see." She takes my arm and gently inspects it. "No bones sticking out. That's a good thing. But there's a bend here where there shouldn't be and some swelling. I think you may have a broken arm."

When I raise an eyebrow to her, she adds, "I took first aid."

I hold my arm by the wrist. Now that I know I've likely broken it, it hurts even more.

Grace wheels around. "I've got to go get that lady out of her van. She hasn't taken her hands off the steering wheel. She may be in shock."

"Can I help?"

"Not unless you have some way to make this snow stop. If this keeps up, we'll get so wet we'll freeze before help arrives."

I smile a little. "I'll see what I can do."

She smiles back at me. Then she jogs to the van. I'm impressed with how confidently she's handling this situation. And I get the feeling she really does like me. For a moment I think living here—*visiting* here, I correct myself—might not be so bad after all. But then I see Jeremy and Eric strolling my way.

Crap. We're way out in the middle of nowhere. It could be twenty minutes or more before help arrives. My arm is broken. And now that the bus driver is out of commission, I'm fair game.

Chapter Nine

My phone buzzes in my pocket, and I keep an eye on Jeremy and Eric as I take it out. Another text from Gran.

What kind of accident? Are you hurt?

I take a photo of the van crashed into the back of the bus and send it to Gran. Then I text with my left hand.

I think my arm is broken.
Where are you?

I call up my location with an app on my phone and send the map to Gran.

She texts again. **I'm on my way.**

Thank God. She's giving me a ride home. At least I won't have to get back on a school bus today.

Then the phone rings. Gran. I answer it. "I'm okay," I tell her.

"I'm in the truck, warming it up. I'll be there in less than ten minutes. What's this about your arm?"

I peer at Jeremy and Eric. Now that I'm talking on the phone, they're standing nearby like they're only hanging out. But I can see they're listening. I turn my back on them as I talk to Gran.

I wiggle my fingers and feel the burn in my arm. "I don't know. It's swollen. It doesn't feel right."

"You really think it's broken?" Gran asks.

"Grace thinks it might be."

"Grace?"

"A girl on the bus."

"We'll let a doctor tell us if it's broken or not."

"Grace has first aid," I say.

"Does she now?"

I watch Grace as she helps the old lady out of the van. "She's nice," I add.

"*Is* she now?"

"She's just a friend," I say.

"I thought you hadn't made any friends," Gran says. But there is a smile in her voice.

"This busload of kids is crazy, Gran. I mean *nuts*. I'm not sure I can do this every day."

"I can't drive you back and forth into town, Mark. I couldn't afford it."

"I know."

"You'll get used to things."

But that's just it. I don't want to get used to things. "Seriously. I don't know if I can do this. Any of this."

"Just sit tight, and I'll be there in no time. I'm on my way."

"Gran?"

"Yes."

"Did Mom really ask about me?"

"Of course she did."

"I mean—" *Does she still care about me?*

"She loves you, honey," Gran says. "You're not to blame. Do you understand? What your mom did had nothing to do with you."

No, I don't understand.

"We'll talk more tonight. I'll be right there." She ends the call.

I pocket my phone and hold my right arm. It hurts even more now.

"So, Mark, what do you say we get back to our little game of truth or dare?"

I swing around. Eric is there, with Jeremy right behind him.

"Why don't we start with the truth?" Eric says. He raises his voice loud enough that all the kids turn to us. "Tell us, why *did* you move up here in the middle of November?"

"It's none of your business."

Grace locks gazes with me as she leads the old woman toward us, like she knows I'm in trouble.

"Your mom gets sick a lot, doesn't she?" Jeremy asks. I can see it on his face. He's going to tell the kids everything.

I push past him. "Leave me alone."

But they follow.

"I hear she's not so much sick as crazy," says Eric.

"Screw off."

"She gets sad, doesn't she?" Eric says. "So sad. She got so sad this time that she tried to off herself, didn't she?"

I face him. "You have no right—"

"She took a bunch of pills to kill herself and ended up in a psych ward."

I feel my eyes sting.

"Oh, he's going to cry," Eric says in a singsong voice. "Now *he's* so sad. So very sad. Such a sad, sad boy."

"Why do you suppose she did that?" Jeremy says in a booming voice. "Tried to kill herself?"

I see one of the little kids' eyes grow large.

"I'm thinking it was to get away from her kid," Eric says. "Because Mark here drove her *crazy*." He laughs a sort of fake, hysterical laugh.

I push the Grim Reaper. Hard. He falls backward into the snow. His hood comes off, revealing a wild mass of black hair. He seems confused for a moment, like he can't quite believe I pushed him. Then he leaps back up and takes a swing at me. But I circle around him and use my left hand to pull his jacket down from behind, so he can't use either arm. He fumbles for a moment, wrestling with the hoodie to free his arms. A bunch of the young kids laugh.

"Get him!" Eric yells.

Jeremy launches himself toward me but slips in the snow. I take off, holding my hurt arm. Eric shakes off his hoodie and isn't far behind. He grabs me by my right arm, the sore arm. I grunt in pain and claw at his hand to get him to let go.

"Stop it!" Grace cries out. She's still holding the old lady's arm. "Mark's hurt. I think his arm is broken. You'll make it worse."

I see a strange look cross Eric's face. He lets go. "I didn't know," he mumbles. I have a flash thought. Maybe he knows what a broken arm feels like. But the moment passes, and his face hardens again. He pushes his finger into my chest. "You made me look like an idiot."

"You did that all by yourself," I say.

"You, you—" Eric's face contorts as he struggles to find the words. Then he leans in so close I can smell the garlic on his breath. "You are *so* dead."

Chapter Ten

Grace helps the old lady settle onto the log, next to Ida. Then she wedges herself between me and Eric. "Aren't things bad enough right now without you pulling this kind of crap?" she asks him. "The little kids are scared after that crash. They don't need to watch a fight too."

Eric ignores her and talks over her head at me. "What?" he says. "You let your girlfriend stand up for you?"

"She's not my girlfriend," I say. But he's got a point. I've got to fight this battle myself or this guy will never leave me alone. I step around Grace and face Eric.

"Okay," I say. "You want to play truth or dare? I'll tell you the truth. About *you*. You try so hard to seem scary. But you're the one who's scared."

Eric lifts his chin. "Oh yeah? And just what am I scared of?"

"Your dad, I'm guessing."

Eric takes a step back like I've slapped him in the face. His eyes dart to the kids watching us.

I push a finger into his chest. "You're scared people will find out just how scared you are. So you wear this, this—" I wave a hand at his Grim Reaper getup. It's a lot like the ones my Gran sells at

Halloween. "This disguise, this *mask*. But this isn't you, *is* it? *You're* the sad, sad boy."

"Mark!" Grace says. "That's enough."

"Maybe my mom did try to take her life to get away from me," I say. "But at least she never beat me up."

"Mark!" Grace says, shocked.

Eric lifts his head. His face contorts, and a tear rolls down his cheek. He quickly wipes it away, smudging his eyeliner. Then he walks away.

Jeremy just stands there, staring at me. I doubt any of these rural kids have ever had the nerve to stand up to him or Eric before. But I've faced worse at my school back in the city.

"Don't you have a girlfriend to go make out with?" I ask him. He shrugs and strides over to Sophia.

I turn, triumphant, expecting Grace to celebrate with me. But I can tell by her face that she's mad.

"That was really mean," she says. "What you said to Eric."

"He got what he deserved. Somebody had to let him know he can't treat people like that. Now he knows what it feels like to be on the other end of the stick."

"You used what I told you in private about him, about his dad."

"But—"

"You really hurt him. And it was a dumb thing to do. I know he was being a jerk, but you shamed him in front of all the kids. Now he's got to save face. He'll find a way to get even."

I look over at Eric. His head is down, covered in that hood. But I can tell he's crying. He's wiping his eyes. Suddenly I feel like a total jerk.

"You're right," I say quietly.

"What?"

"I said, you're right."

Neither of us talks for a minute. Then I say, "The train hasn't arrived."

Grace shrugs. "I guess they stopped it."

"Or it had already gone by before we got here," I say.

Grace puts a hand on my shoulder, and her voice softens. "Is it true? What Eric said about your mom? That she tried to take her own life?"

I feel a surge of anger. "What do you care?" I yell. But then I see Grace's shocked expression. "I'm sorry," I say. "I just—I didn't want anyone to know. Now everybody knows. Or they will after all these kids pass it on."

Grace hugs herself. "I was only asking because…maybe I have some idea what that feels like."

She's standing here in the falling snow with no coat. I take off my puffy jacket and wrap it around her.

"Your mom had a stroke," I say. "That's not the same."

"No, it's not. But the stroke changed Mom for a while. It changed her behavior. She got mad a lot, and cried a lot, over nothing. I was never sure how she was going to act. Like, she was someone else. And she was always tired. She never had any energy for me." She paused. "For a long time I felt like I had lost my mom."

I rub my sore arm. I'm covered in goose bumps now. "My mom is always tired too, when she's down."

"Depression?"

"She's bipolar. Sometimes she's so up, she's wild. She talks really fast and stays up all night sewing dresses. Crazy dresses that no one will wear. And she'll dance and dance."

"She sounds kind of fun."

"But then she crashes, and she can't get out of bed. She cries over everything, she hates herself. This last time she crashed so bad. She gave up on her life." I shiver. "I felt like she gave up on me."

Grace steps close to me and lifts my coat over my shoulders so it covers both of us. "So what Eric said about your mom trying to kill herself to get away from you—"

"It hit home, because when Mom took all those pills, that's exactly what I felt. I thought Mom had gotten tired of me. She didn't want our life. She just wanted to leave."

"But that's not it at all, is it?" Grace says. "She's sick, just like my mom was sick. The chemical imbalance in your mom's brain makes her feel that way, like nothing matters. But that's not her—that's the illness. Like my mom's anger wasn't her. It was a symptom of her brain injury, the stroke."

"Yeah, I guess. But it doesn't feel that way. It feels like it's my fault."

"I know. I used to blame myself when Mom got mad for no reason. I thought there was something wrong with me. That I must be doing something to make her mad. But it wasn't me at all. It was the stroke, the damage it had done to her brain. Now…"

"Now?"

"Things are better," she says. "But I know they will never be the same, you know? That makes me sad sometimes." She takes my hand. "Things will get better for you too," she says. "Your mom *will* get better."

"But it will be a long haul," I say, thinking of Gran's text.

"What's that?"

"It's going to be a while before Mom really does get better. And I'm stuck here until she does." At that school, on this bus. Out in the middle of nowhere.

"Is that really so bad?" she says, bumping my shoulder with hers. "There are worse places."

"Really?" I grin. "Worse than this bus?"

She laughs. "Maybe not." She looks down and kicks at the snow at her feet. "But I wouldn't mind if you stayed. I mean, if you had to."

My phone buzzes. A message from my mom this time.

Heard you had an adventure!

Followed by a smiley face. Mom's trying to sound upbeat, happy, even though I know she's not. I haven't talked to her since the ambulance came to take her away. Gran must have phoned her while she warmed up the truck.

You should phone her, Gran said. But I'm not sure I'm ready to. I still feel angry, hurt. Mom tried to leave me in the worst kind of way. But I guess I can start with a text.

My arm is sore, but I'll be okay.

I look up at the snowflakes coming down and feel the warmth of Grace beside me. And for the first time since I found Mom on the floor, I feel like it's the truth. I *will* be okay.

My phone vibrates. Mom again.

How was your first day at school?

All right, I guess.

Settled in?

I scan the scene around me. Eric is sitting off by himself. Grace is huddled next to me under my jacket. The younger kids have settled down and are chatting with each other. Jeremy is even clowning around with the little princess, wearing her crown and pulling faces to make her and the other kindies laugh. The snow has collected on the trees. It's pretty. Christmas-card pretty. Away from the noise of the city and the noise of the bus, I suddenly feel peaceful.

Yeah.

Maybe I *am* starting to settle in.

I miss you.

I stare down at my phone for a long minute. For some stupid reason those three little words from Mom make me cry. I wipe away the tears, hoping Grace will think I'm just wiping off snowflakes.

I miss you too, Mom.

Grace nudges me. "Hey, here's your ride home. Your gran beat the ambulance." Just as she says that, I hear the ambulance siren blaring in the distance. The bus to pick up the kids won't be far behind.

I watch as Gran's truck slowly creeps down the slippery hill. Her 4x4 pickup is way better on the road than the old lady's van. But she's not taking any chances.

"Make sure you get that arm checked out," Grace tells me as she hands me my coat. "*Today*."

"I will."

Crap. I just realized that means I'll have to drive all the way back into town with Gran. I shoulder my backpack and start shuffling through the snow to the road.

"Hey, Mark."

I turn back to Grace.

Now, without my coat, she's hugging herself again. "Remember how I said my mom forced me to move here when she remarried?"

"Yeah."

"It took me a long time to get used to the idea that I *was* here. But when I did, things got better. When I stopped fighting it, all this didn't seem so bad. And I started to make friends."

"These kids are your *friends*?" I say.

"Not these kids," she says. "Any kid who takes this bus is *crazy*." She smiles, and my heart leaps again. I grin back at her. And I know that I do, in fact, have at least one friend here.

Chapter Eleven

The next day is bright and sunny. The snow has melted. It's almost like the snowfall and accident never happened. Except I've got proof right here that it did. My arm is encased in a cast. Gran took me to the hospital right after she picked me up at the accident site. Grace was right. I do have a fracture. No big deal, but I'll be wearing this cast for the next few weeks. It's kind of a pain. I can't write properly, and the cast keeps getting in my way. As I get on the bus for the ride to school, it knocks against the door. Ouch. That stings.

This new bus smells like industrial cleaner. No dried pudding on the ceiling either. There's a new driver sitting up front. He's big and meaty, like a coach or an ex-cop. Handpicked for this particular busload of kids, I bet. "Is Ida okay?" I ask him.

"She's still in the hospital," he says. "But I'm sure she'll be all right."

"Is she coming back? Is she going to drive our route again?"

"Let's just say she needs a holiday from you guys."

I snort out a small laugh. "I hear ya."

I scan the bus for Grace. She isn't sitting at the front with the little kids. I worry for a moment that she isn't on the bus today. No sign of Jeremy. But then

I spot her. She's sitting in the middle of the bus. She's in the seat just in front of Chucky Cheese. She waves, inviting me to sit with her.

But the kindergarten girl in the front seat stops me before I can head down the aisle. She's wearing the princess outfit again today. It's a bit worse for wear after yesterday's "adventure." Her tiara's a little crooked. "Can I sign your arm?" she asks.

"Sure," I say, holding out my cast.

"Not now," the driver says. "Find a seat. I've got to get you to school."

But the younger kids start swarming down the aisle to sign my arm, and the driver gives up. He stays parked where he is for the moment, at the foot of Gran's driveway. Farther down the aisle, I see Eric stand too. I keep an eye on him as I hold my cast out for everyone to sign. If the Grim Reaper is coming my way, I'm pretty sure it isn't to sign my cast.

I work my way down the aisle toward Grace. But the kids in nearly every seat stop me, wanting to sign my cast. I guess I'm officially a member of this sad little school-bus community now.

Grace smiles and slides over in her seat as I reach her. She's not wearing her glasses today. She must have contacts in. And she's wearing her hair down. It cascades in waves over her shoulders. She doesn't seem nerdy at all today. She's, like, *hot*. My face reddens at the thought.

"You're not going to barf, are you?" I ask her. Then cringe. That didn't come out right.

"Pardon me?" she asks.

"I mean, you said you get carsick. You said that's why you sit up front."

"I get carsick when I read on the bus," she says. "I usually read to shut out all this." She waves a hand at the chaos around us. "But you're here, so we can talk instead."

I'm about to sit when Eric slaps me on the back to stop me.

"Hey," he says.

"Uh, hey?" I respond.

His black hood is pulled low over his face. He's wearing dark-purple lipstick today. That's about all I can see of him. "About yesterday," he says. "My grandma heard about our fight from your grandma. She thought I should apologize."

"Oh?" It doesn't sound like Eric thinks he should. "I guess I should too," I say. "I shouldn't have said that stuff about your dad or your fashion sense."

He glances sideways at the kids around us who are listening in. "Yeah, well."

"I didn't think you'd be on the bus today," I tell Eric. "Ida said she was going to give you a third memo."

"I guess with the crash and all, she forgot about it. And I wasn't going to say anything." He steps so close that I get a good look at the zit on the side of his nose. "You're not going to say anything, are you?"

"Ah, no."

He reaches in his pocket, and I cringe. I'm sure he's pulling out his lighter to set my cast on fire or something. But instead he holds out a red Sharpie. "You cool with this?" he asks. He points the pen at my arm.

"I guess," I say nervously. If he writes something nasty about me on my cast, I don't know how I'll clean it off. But I can see the two cavemen eyeing me from their seats behind him, like I better do what Eric asks. I hold out my cast for Eric to sign, expecting the worst.

But Eric starts doodling flames up my cast, like the kind you'd see on a hot rod or something. "Hey, that's pretty good," I say, admiring the artwork once he finishes.

Sometimes people surprise you.

He shrugs. "I draw," he says. He pulls out a sketchbook and shows me his latest, a pencil drawing of yesterday's accident. The front end of the van is all bent up against the back of the bus, like it was in the accident. There's Ida and the old lady sitting on the log. The kids waiting in the clearing. And there's me and Grace in the middle of it all, standing together, sharing a coat. I mean, I can tell it's me and Grace in the drawing.

"That's really good," I say. I see his purple lips curve into a little smile. Then he lifts his head so I can see his eyes. "Maybe you should draw instead of setting things on fire," I add.

"Maybe."

"Or we could do both," one of the cavemen says. "You draw, and I'll set your pictures on fire." He snatches Eric's drawing and pulls out a lighter.

Eric launches himself over the seat to grab it back. They tussle there until the bus driver hollers for them to stop. When they don't, the driver stomps down the aisle to seize the lighter.

As he passes, the cheese kid pelts the back of the driver's head with cheese curds. Before the driver turns, scowling, Chucky plunks back down in his seat and pretends he hasn't done anything. Another kid tries to squirt yogurt at Chucky, hitting the driver in the arm. The driver wipes off his sleeve and roars at the kids behind us.

I look at Grace. She just raises an eyebrow in that way that says, *Can you believe this*? Then she pats the seat beside her, and I sit just in time to get a splat of yogurt in the back of my head. I wipe it off, then rub it on my jeans. Wonderful. The faint smell of melting upholstery is in the air. Either Eric or the cavemen have been at it again, burning holes in the seats. Some kid is flying a drone around the bus. Half the kids are screaming and yelling. The new driver is yelling in response. Chucky Cheese hurls cheese curds at the yogurt girls. And, yup, out come the pudding packs. The start of just another ride on a rural school bus. But somehow it all doesn't seem so threatening today. Today it just feels like a party.

Acknowledgments

I rode a rural school bus. And I was the weird kid too. The food fights, the vinyl seat burning, the yelling and screaming, the name calling and stressed-out bus drivers. I remember it all. So I'd like to thank the kids who were willing to chat with me about their school-bus experiences. Anyone who regularly endures those long bus rides home deserves a medal.

I'd also like to acknowledge Lorraine Robbins, who wrote a graduate studies project called *Views From a School Bus Window: Stories of the Children Who Ride*. Lorraine's account of her project, where she interviewed rural bus riders in Alberta, backed up the experiences I heard about from the rural bus riders I talked to, as well as those I experienced myself many years ago.

Gail Anderson-Dargatz is an award-winning author of over a dozen books, including *The Cure for Death by Lightning* and *A Recipe for Bees*, which were finalists for the Scotiabank Giller Prize. She also teaches other authors how to write fiction. Gail lives in the Shuswap region of British Columbia.

Another **Orca currents** by **Gail Anderson-Dargatz**

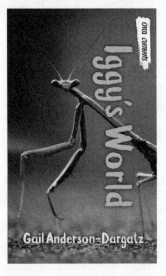

Eager to prove himself to his famous family, Iggy starts his own podcast about what interests him: insects.

It's not until Iggy embarrasses his sister on air that his podcast really takes off. He's thrilled with his own success until she fires back. Now it's all-out war.

Take a sneak peek into *Iggy's World*

Episode One

Testing, testing. One, two, three. Is the mic on my phone working? Check, check. I'll have to keep my voice down. My dad's filming a show right now. I'm recording this podcast just off the set.

Here we go! Welcome to *Iggy's World.*

Hi! I'm your host, Iggy Zambini, and you're listening to episode one of *Iggy's*

World, a podcast about insects. I know, I know. Insects make your skin crawl. But don't tune out yet. This podcast isn't *just* about bugs. For example, today I'm recording this from the set of the sci-fi web series *Great Big Bugs in Space*. Because, you know, the show is about great big *bugs* in space.

My dad, Jove Zambini, is the director of the show. Maybe you've heard of him. He produced and directed the mystery web series *In a Pickle: The Pickle Factory Murders*. Okay, maybe you didn't hear about that one. What about *Sock Knitters' Showdown*? It's a reality show about knitters competing to make the best socks. Heard of that one? Yeah, I'm guessing not.

But Dad's latest project is a hit, sort of. At least, it has a small cult following. People like to watch *Great Big Bugs in Space* because it's so cheesy. The costumes and sets are super cheap and corny. I can see a guy over in the corner dressed as a giant beetle. Mom made his shell from a tinfoil roasting pan. She bought it at the dollar store and spray-painted it black.

That's kind of Mom and Dad's thing, making web series on a shoestring budget. On this show, Dad not only directs but is also the lead actor. Mom makes all the costumes and props and writes the scripts too. And Dad just gave my sister, Cara, a part on the series. Funny, he never offered *me* a part.

The series is crowd-funded. That means people go to a website and offer money so Dad can make the shows. But he never gets a lot of cash that way—at least, not the kind of big bucks producers usually need to make a TV show. That's why Dad is making a web series, a kind of mini TV show on the internet. They're a lot cheaper to produce.

And that's also why Dad is filming the show at the bike park near our house. He doesn't have to pay to build a set. Quite a few big-budget movies have been filmed in our area though. The hills are dry and covered in sagebrush and ponderosa pine. Filmmakers can pretend the landscape of this part of British Columbia is somewhere in the United States or Mexico.

There are spots here that could also pass for another planet. That makes this a perfect setting for a sci-fi flick. But it's still weird to see actors dressed as insects hanging out in *my* bike park.

"CUT! Iggy, what are you doing?"

Oh, crap. That's my dad, yelling as he marches over here. I don't think he's too happy with me.

"Whatever I did, Dad, I didn't mean to." I'm nearly six feet tall, but I still have to look up a little when I'm talking to him.

"Iggy, you know better than to talk while we're filming."

"Sorry, Dad. I'm recording my first episode of *Iggy's World* and—"

"Your first episode of what?"

"*Iggy's World.* My new show."

"A show? What, like your sister's?"

"Sort of. Only hers is a vlog, remember?" My sister has her own online TV show.

"Of course, I know about Cara's YouTube channel. But who are *you* talking to?"

"My phone, Dad. I'm recording a podcast. I have to fill in stuff for my listeners."

"You're recording *right now*? But where is your microphone?"

Dad is so old school. "I don't need a mic, Dad. I've got a voice-recorder app on my phone. In fact, this app is *made* for recording podcasts. I just hit *Record* and create my show. Then I hit a button to publish it, and the app uploads my show to a bunch of sites."

"What's this show of yours about exactly?"

"It's about insects."

"Of course it is. What *else* would it be about?" My dad rolls his eyes.

"Why do you say it like that?"

"Iggy, you never stop talking about bugs. I get that it's your thing, but for the rest of us it's—"

"Boring! I know."

"And aren't you just a little old for this kind of hobby, Iggy? I understood your interest in bugs when you were in fourth grade, but now that you're fourteen—"

See what I have to put up with around here? I don't get any support for my stuff. Nobody cares. Not even my dad.